GELERT
A Man's Best Friend

Cerys Matthews
Illustrated by Fran Evans

Pont

This is a centuries-old story from Wales. Through the tale of a loyal dog fending off a vicious wolf, it warns of the dangers of jumping to conclusions and acting in haste. Similar folk tales are also found in other cultures. In India, for example, a black snake takes the place of the wolf, and a mongoose, the dog; in Malaysia the wolf is a tiger and the dog is a tame bear. These stories have been told for generations to teach youngsters good lessons in life as part of ancient fireside lore. I hope you'll enjoy, despite maybe shedding a tear or two.

Faster than lightning a prince, dog and steed
return to the castle at breathtaking speed.

'My lady, my lady, I must go away,
but Gelert will guard you all night and all day.'

'Fine,' Siwan trills and their baby boy smiles.
They feel quite safe with this hound at their side.

While Gelert so gently and quietly creeps,
the princess rocks babe, till the babe falls asleep.

'I must go to supper. Stay watchful! Wait here!
Let no one disturb him, let nobody near!'

But what is that shadow? A beast on the prowl?
A hungry black wolf! How he skulks . . . how he scowls.

A wolf in the bedroom! Just look at his size —
and he's looking at baby with bloodthirsty eyes . . .

UP , Gelert, UP!

How they fight and they howl!
They slash and they gnash.
They gnarl and they growl.

They snarl and they bite, and they heave and they roar.

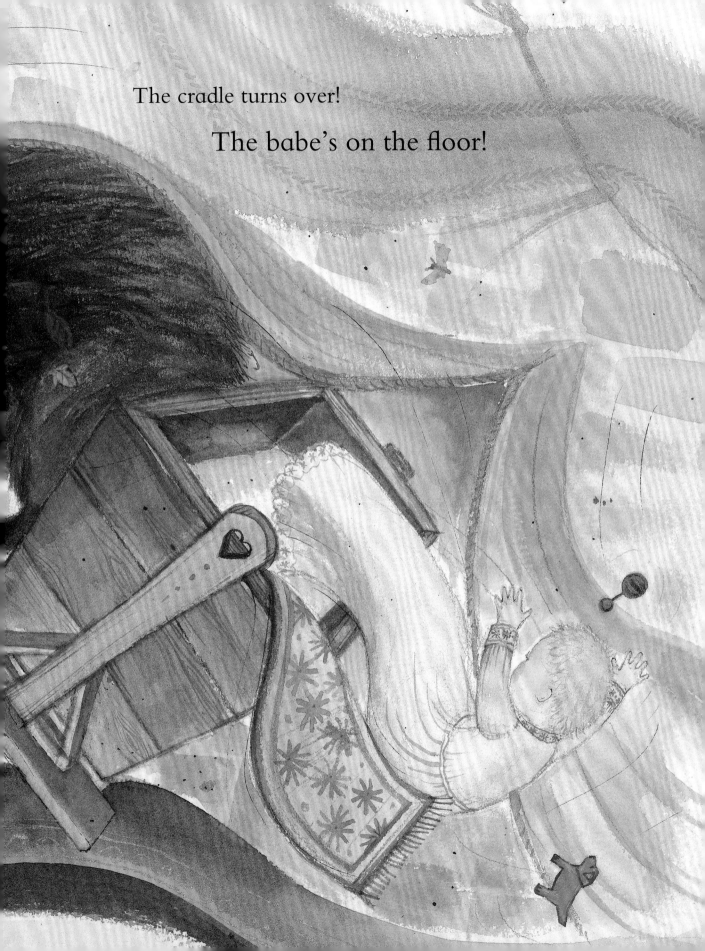

The cradle turns over!

The babe's on the floor!

Wolf's hiss is so monstrous, so savage, so foul.
'I'm hungry! Where's baby? I want him right now!'

The moment has come. Gelert strikes at his head,
a powerful blow – and the wolf is now dead.

The dog is exhausted. Llywelyn the Great
returns from his travels – but is he too late?

The cradle is empty. 'Hound! What have you done?
Why are you blood-stained? Oh no! my poor son!'

The Prince lifts his sword. He knows he must kill
his faithful dog Gelert, so trusting and still.

A stab. And then silence. And then a faint cry.
The Prince lifts the sheets . . .

. . . the baby's alive!

So when the wolf's body is found lying near,
the truth of what happened is horribly clear.

'Oh, Gelert, I'm sorry,' the Prince cries in pain,
'I'll never forget. You have not died in vain!'

The Prince buries Gelert – a dignified end:
'Let the world always know that you were my friend!'

Look up in the sky, on a dark winter's night.
It's Gelert you'll find . . . in the stars shining bright.

For Silverfox ~ C. M.

For Moss and Twm, my faithful hounds ~ F. E.

Published in Wales in 2014 by Pont Books, an imprint of Gomer Press,
Llandysul, Ceredigion, SA44 4JL
www.gomer.co.uk

ISBN 978 1 84851 464 5
Reprinted 2017, 2018

A CIP record for this title is available from the British Library.

This book is published with the financial support of the Welsh Books Council.

Printed and bound in Wales at Gomer Press, Llandysul, Ceredigion